My Treasure Hunt TROUBLE!

BETTY G. BIRNEY

Illustrated by Penny Dann

faber and faber

To Humphrey's GREAT-GREAT-GREAT

friend, Julia Heydon-Wells

First published in 2011
by Faber and Faber Limited
Bloomsbury House, 74–77 Great Russell Street,
London WC1B 3DA

Printed in England by CPI Cox & Wyman, Reading

A CIP record for this book
is available from the British Library

ISBN 978–0–956–62763–6

2 4 6 8 10 9 7 5 3 1

WELCOME TO MY WORLD

Hi! I'm Humphrey. I'm lucky to be the classroom hamster in Room 26 of Longfellow School. It's a big job because I have to go home with a different student each weekend and try to help my friends. Luckily, my cage has a lock-that-doesn't-lock, so I can get out and have BIG-BIG-BIG adventures!

I'd like you to meet some of my friends

Og

a frog, is the other classroom pet in Room 26. He makes a funny sound: BOING!

Mrs Brisbane

is our teacher. She really understands her students – even me!

Lower-Your-Voice-A.J.

has a loud voice and calls me Humphrey Dumpty.

Wait-For-The-Bell Garth

is A.J.'s best friend and a good friend of mine, too.

Speak-Up-Sayeh
is unsqueakably smart, but she's shy
and doesn't like to speak in class.

Golden-Miranda
has golden hair, like I do. She also
has a dog named Clem. Eeek!

Stop-Giggling-Gail
loves to giggle – and so do I!

Sit-Still-Seth
is a friend who's always on
the move.

I think you'll like my other friends, too, such as
Don't-Complain-Mandy, Pay-Attention-Art,
Raise-Your-Hand-Heidi and *Repeat-It-Please-Richie.*

CONTENTS

Secret Treasure

'Can you keep a secret, Humphrey?' Garth whispered.

'Of course,' I whispered back.

But since I'm a hamster and Garth is a human, all he heard was 'Squeak!'

'How about you, Og?' Garth asked my friend.

Og answered 'BOING!' because he is a frog who makes a VERY-VERY-VERY strange sound.

'There's going to be a treasure hunt in my garden tomorrow,' Garth said. 'But it's a

1

secret. Don't tell anybody, okay?'

'Eeek!' I squeaked. I wasn't sure what a treasure hunt was, but it sounded exciting.

'BOING-BOING!' Og splashed around in his tank.

'I've worked out some of the clues already,' Garth said. 'And I haven't even told A.J.'

A.J. was Garth's best friend. They were both in my class at Longfellow School.

I'm the classroom hamster in Room 26. Og is the classroom frog.

It's part of my job to go home with a different student each weekend.

Frogs can go for several days without food, so Og usually stays back in Room 26. But this weekend Garth invited everyone in our class to a party, including Og and me. Our teacher, Mrs Brisbane, said we could

3

both go, which made me unsqueakably happy.

My cage and Og's tank sat on the desk in Garth's room. We watched as he cut paper into squares.

'The clues should be hard,' he said. 'But not too hard. After all, somebody has to find the treasure.'

'What's the treasure?' I asked, wishing Garth could understand me.

Garth stopped cutting paper and looked at me.

'Thanks, Humphrey,' he said. 'You gave me an idea for a great place to hide it!'

'You're welcome,' I squeaked. 'But what *is* the treasure?'

'BOING!' Og said.

As Garth began writing on the squares of paper, I thought about TREASURE-

TREASURE-TREASURE! I knew that treasure was something special, like gold and silver coins. Or sparkly jewels.

In the books Mrs Brisbane read to us in class, people were always looking for treasure. Sometimes treasure was buried in the ground. Sometimes it was at the bottom of the sea.

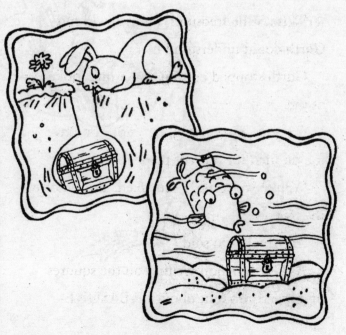

I scurried to the side of my cage near Og's tank.

'What kind of treasure would you like?' I asked him.

Og just stared at me with his goofy eyes. I didn't think coins or jewels would be of much use to a frog. He'd probably rather have crickets or flies. *Ewww!*

Coins or jewels wouldn't be of use to a hamster, either, but I still wanted to go on the treasure hunt.

Suddenly, a small voice called out, 'Ham!'

Garth's little brother, Andy, raced into the room and headed for my cage.

'He's a hamster, not a ham,' Garth said.

'Ham!' Andy shouted.

I don't like being called a 'ham', but, to be fair, Andy is quite small.

Andy pointed at the squares of paper. 'What's that?'

'That's where I'm writing down clues for the treasure hunt,' Garth explained.

'What's that?' Andy asked.

'It's a game where my friends have to follow clues and see who can find the treasure first,' Garth said.

'What's that?'
Andy asked,
pointing at Og.
'That's
Og the frog,'
Garth said.
'Now be quiet
so I can write out the
clues.'

'What's—' said Andy.

Garth put his finger to his lips and said,
'Sssh!'

Andy put his finger to his lips and said,
'Sssh!' too.

Garth wrote something on one of the
squares.

'Frog,' Andy said.

He stared hard at Og. Og stared right
back.

'BOING!' Og said in his funny voice.

'Sssh!' Andy said.

Og leaped
into the water
with a huge
splash.

Garth
sighed.

'Mum!' he
called. 'Can
you get Andy out of here? He's bothering
me.'

Garth's mum appeared at the door. 'Let
Andy help. He wants to be included in the
party.'

'I can't write out the clues with him here,'
Garth complained.

'You can only stay if you watch quietly,'
Garth's mum told Andy.

She put her finger to her lips and said, 'Sssh!'

'Okay,' the little boy answered. 'Sssh!'

At first, Andy watched quietly as Garth began writing on the slips of paper.

'What rhymes with flower?' Garth asked.

'BOING!' Og said.

Poor Og. Doesn't he know that BOING doesn't rhyme with flower at all?

'Shower! That works,' Garth said.

I was trying to think of a flower that showered when Andy asked, 'What's that?'

'A clue,' Garth told him. 'Like a riddle.'

'Widdle,' Andy said.

Aha! A clue is like a riddle! I like riddles. I was unsqueakably curious about these clues.

Garth wrote some more and then asked me, 'What do you think of this clue?' and he read it out loud:

'Everyone knows you must water a flower. Tip me over, I'll give it a shower.'

'GREAT-GREAT-GREAT!' I squeaked. I had no idea what the answer to the riddle was.

As Garth wrote, he muttered other strange words, like 'frown' and 'goal' and 'basket'.

Then he opened a desk drawer and pulled out a treasure chest so small that he could hold it in the palm of his hand. Still, it looked like a real treasure chest and it even had a tiny lock on it.

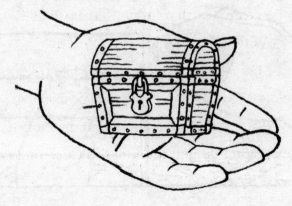

'What's that?' Andy said.

'It's the treasure for the treasure hunt. It's something anyone in Room 26 would love to have,' Garth said.

Anyone? Even a hamster?

'Remember, this is a secret,' he added. 'Do you promise not to tell anyone?'

'Promise,' Andy said.

'Promise,' I squeaked.

'BOING!' Og agreed.

To my surprise, Garth opened the door to my cage!

Then he carefully put the treasure chest inside, covering it over with my bedding.

'You leave it right there, Humphrey,' he said. 'And don't peek.'

'Okay,' I promised.

But even as I said it, I knew it would be a hard promise to keep.

The Trouble Begins

'A.J.'s here,' Garth's dad called from the hallway.

Garth quickly hid all of the pieces of paper in his desk drawer.

'He's spending the night,' he explained. 'But don't tell him about the treasure hunt.'

'Okay,' Andy said. 'Sssh!'

A.J. raced into the room. 'Hi, Humphrey Dumpty,' he said.

He calls me Humphrey Dumpty for fun.

I call him Lower-Your-Voice-A.J. because of his loud voice.

14

'Hi, Og,' A.J. said.

Og answered with a friendly, 'BOING!'

'BOING-BOING!' Andy said.

Then he hopped across the room,
shouting, 'BOING-BOING! I'M A FROG!'

'Quiet, Andy,' Garth told him.

A.J. leaned down close to Andy and said,
'Sssh!'

Andy said, 'Sssh!'

'Bedtime, Andy,' Garth's dad called from
the hallway.

Andy said, 'Night-night, ham and frog.'

The boys played a game until Garth's dad called from the hallway again.

'Time to get washed and ready for bed, guys,' he said. 'You've got a big day tomorrow.'

Once Garth and A.J. had left, I told Og, 'We've got a big day tomorrow, too.'

This time, Og was silent.

Maybe he wished the treasure was in his tank instead of my cage.

I wanted to uncover the treasure to see what was inside, but I'd promised Garth I wouldn't peek.

It's always a good idea to keep a promise. I hopped on my wheel so I wouldn't think about the treasure.

I was spinning FAST-FAST-FAST when I saw the door to my cage open.

I wanted to see who was opening it, but my wheel was going so fast, I had to wait until it slowed down. While I waited, I saw the shadowy shape of a hand reach in and poke around the cage.

I had to see whose hand it was, so I hopped off the wheel and flipped head-over-paws across my bedding.

I must have been dizzy because everything was still spinning.

The hand picked up the small treasure chest. I tried to see whose hand it was, but now the chest blocked my view.

'Stop!' I squeaked as loudly

as a small hamster can squeak. 'Stop right now!'

'Sssh!' was the only answer.

'Stop, thief!' I squeaked as my heart went THUMP-THUMP-THUMP.

No one answered. But I did smell something. Was it . . . chocolate?

'BOING-BOING!' Og called out as he splashed wildly in his tank.

Before I knew it, the hand had taken the treasure chest out of my cage and closed the door. I dashed forward to see who it was but it was too late. Garth's room was empty.

'Og, did you see the thief?' I asked.

Og didn't answer this time. I don't think he'd seen who it was. Neither had I.

I was unsqueakably upset.

The treasure chest was GONE-GONE-GONE!

'A thief was here!' I told Garth when he and A.J. came back, ready for bed. 'We have to find the thief!'

'Calm down, Humphrey Dumpty,' A.J. said. 'Sssh!'

'Goodnight, Humphrey,' Garth said.

He took off his glasses and got into his bed. A.J. got into the other bed in Garth's room.

'BOING-BOING!' Og said.

'Goodnight, Og,' Garth said.

I love humans but sometimes I wish they'd pay a little more attention.

The boys talked in the dark for a while. And soon I could tell by their breathing that they were asleep. But *I* didn't sleep the whole night.

Like most hamsters, I am usually wide

awake at night. But I'm not usually so
WORRIED-WORRIED-WORRIED.

It had been nice to have the treasure chest
in my cage. But it was *not nice at all* to have it
missing.

I imagined what would happen the next
day. Everyone would try to find out where
the treasure was by reading Garth's clues.
One of my friends would be the first to get to
my cage. But when that friend got there, the
treasure would be missing.

I thought about how the winner would be
disappointed.

I thought about how Garth would be
disappointed.

Garth's parents would be disappointed, too.

But nobody would be more disappointed
than me.

★

Early the next morning, Garth woke up A.J.

'Come on,' he said. 'We've got to get ready for the party. I've got a big surprise planned.'

'What is it?' A.J. asked.

'Wait and see,' Garth said.

Later, while A.J. was out of the room, I tried to tell Garth again that the treasure was missing.

'You sound excited, Humphrey,' he said. 'So am I! After all, you're the most important guest because you have the treasure!'

Except, of course, I hadn't.

The boys went downstairs to get ready for the party. 'I've got to do something, don't you think?' I asked Og.

'BOING-BOING-BOING!' he agreed.

Since the family was at home, I didn't dare go far from my cage. I decided to search for *new* treasure so the party wouldn't be ruined.

It's a secret, but I have a lock-that-doesn't-lock on my cage door. I can get in and out without any humans knowing it.

I jiggled the lock and the door opened. I was free!

It's a LONG-LONG-LONG way down

to the floor for a small hamster and I didn't have much time. So I decided to stay close to my cage and explore the top of Garth's desk first.

There was a *lot* to see on the top of Garth's desk.

The first thing I saw was a cup full of pencils.

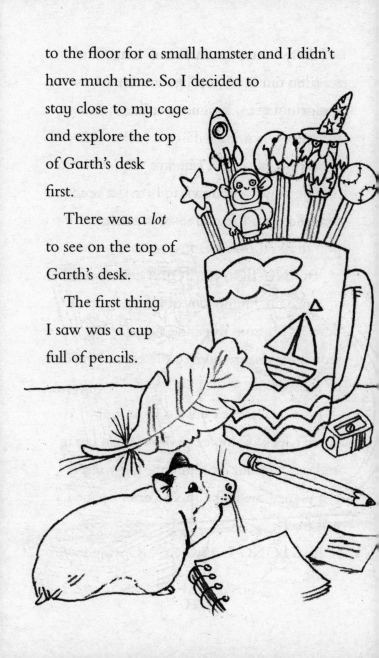

But these weren't plain pencils. They had amazing things on top, like an orange pumpkin head, a smiling monkey, a shiny star. One pencil looked like a rocket ship!

Next to the pencil cup was a huge yellow smiling face. When I saw it, I smiled back.

'Hello,' I said, trying to be friendly.

Then I saw that the smiling face was really a clock.

'Never mind!' I said.

Behind the clock was a frame made of twigs with a picture of Garth and A.J. in it.

I wandered past a deck of cards and ran right into a tiny pink pig. The pig fell over and let out an 'Oink!'

'Sorry,' I said, and quickly moved on.

There were pads of paper, a large blue feather and a pencil box with the planets on it. I know about planets from our lessons in Room 26.

I kept on walking and found myself face to face with a row of big dinosaurs with very large teeth. They weren't real dinosaurs, thank goodness. But they still were unsqueakably scary to a small hamster like me.

I scurried past a row of toy cars in bright colours. One was painted a shiny red and had no roof. It was just my size and I stopped to look at it.

I just touched the shiny red car with my paw when, suddenly, it lurched forward.

'VROOOM!' the car roared.

'Eeek!' I squeaked.

The car zipped across the desk, making wild turns. I ran for my life, zig-zagging ahead of it until I saw I was running straight towards the end of the desk! And it was a LONG-LONG-LONG way down to the floor.

To my left, was a pencil case that was taller than I am.

To my right, was the *front* edge of the desk. Eeek!

At the last second, I leaped up onto the pencil case. The car zoomed past me and flew off the end of the desk. It sailed through the air and then landed on Garth's soft bed.

'BOING-BOING!' Og said as I caught my breath.

My heart was pounding, but I told him, 'Don't worry. I'm fine and so is the car!'

'BOING-BOING-BOING!' Og warned me.

He was right. I didn't have much time.

'I'll hurry,' I told him.

Then something caught my eye. Something shiny and gold, like treasure. It was a coin!

I hopped off the pencil case and scampered towards it. When I sniffed it, I realised that it wasn't a real coin, but a chocolate wrapped in gold paper.

Still, it was shiny and gold and my friends all like chocolate.

I held it in my mouth, careful not to bite down and make teeth marks, and hurried back to my cage.

Og splashed loudly and called out, 'BOING-BOING!'

'I'll tell you all about it,' I said. But I didn't have time because I heard footsteps.

I dashed inside my cage and pulled the door closed behind me.

I slipped the chocolate coin under my bedding just as Garth came in.

'Time to go downstairs,' Garth said. 'The party's about to start.'

The Hunt Is On

Garth and his dad carried my cage and Og's tank outside to a table under a large umbrella.

'A.J., could you come and help me ice the cake?' Garth's mum asked. 'You can lick the spoon.'

'Yes, ma'am,' said A.J.

Once he was gone, Garth said, 'We have to hide the clues before he comes back.'

Og and I watched as Garth and his dad put the little squares of paper all round the garden.

They put them in odd places, like a
watering can and a little red wagon.

'Hurry, Dad,' Garth said.

Suddenly, I heard happy voices. My
friends from Room 26 had arrived!

'Oh, Humphrey, I'm
so glad you're here!'
That was the voice
of Miranda Golden.
I thought of her as
Golden-Miranda
because her hair was as golden as my fur.

'Hi, Humphrey! Hi, Og!'
a giggly voice said.

That had to be Stop-
Giggling-Gail. It was
hard for her to stop
giggling once she got
started.

'HI-HI-HI!' I answered.

Once the guests had arrived, Garth's mum called them into the garden for a funny race. First, each of my friends stood in a sack. Then they had to hold on to the sack while they hopped to the finish line.

I wish Og could have been in that race. He's GREAT-GREAT-GREAT at hopping.

But Gail and her friend Heidi Hopper were good at hopping, too. They won the race.

Next, my friends split up into pairs and Garth's parents tied one kid's right leg to the other kid's left leg. Then they had to work together to run to the finish line. It was unsqueakably funny to see them try to run like that!

Seth and Tabitha won. They are good friends who are both good at sport.

There were other games, too, but it was hard for me to enjoy them. All I could think about was the treasure hunt.

Finally, Garth announced that the hunt would begin. 'There's *real treasure* for the first person who finds it,' he explained.

That was true. It just wasn't the treasure Garth had planned on.

Garth read out the first clue. 'Everyone knows you must water a flower. Tip me over, I'll give it a shower.'

My friends raced off in different directions.

'Og, I saw him put a clue in the watering can,' I squeaked. 'That must be it.'

I was right. Mandy, Richie and Seth all ran to the watering can at the same time.

Mandy reached in and pulled out the next clue.

'The sun is hot, as you will see. You'll be cooler under me.'

There were squeals of excitement as everyone raced to the umbrella over the table I was on.

A.J. had to stand on a chair to reach the next clue and read it.

'You'll find that you will never frown. If you let me go up and down.'

It took a little longer this time for my friends to solve that riddle, but I quickly got it.

'The swing!' I squeaked.

I don't think they understood me, but they all ran to the swing at the back of the garden.

Tabitha grabbed the clue first and read it.

'If going places is your goal, use me, for I am ready to roll!'

'It's the car,' Art shouted.

Art and some of my other friends headed for the driveway. But Heidi and Gail ran towards a little red wagon.

'That's it!' I shouted.

'BOING–BOING!' Og agreed.

Heidi reached into the wagon and pulled out the next clue.

'A-tisket, a-tasket. The last clue's in a basket.'

I must not have been paying attention when Garth and his dad hid that clue. I looked out at the garden.

I was confused. So were my friends.

A.J. and Richie ran towards a large plant in a basket. But when they reached in, there was no clue.

Miranda hurried to Garth's bicycle, which had a wire basket on the front. But when she reached in, there was no clue.

Seth and Tabitha ran to a basket of fruit on the food table. They searched and searched but there was no clue.

My friends all stopped and looked around the garden again.

Then Art spotted a tiny basket hanging from a low tree branch. He reached inside and found the clue, which he read.

'You'll find the treasure – do not worry. Look for something cute and furry.'

My heart went THUMP-THUMP-THUMP. This time *I* was the clue.

At first, my friends just stood there. I could tell they were thinking hard.

A.J. picked up Andy's teddy bear from a chair. He looked and looked but there was no treasure.

'Cute and furry,' I heard Miranda whisper to Sayeh.

Suddenly, Sayeh's face lit up. I call her Speak-Up-Sayeh because she's so quiet in class. But this time her voice was loud and clear as she said, 'Humphrey!'

Sayeh and Miranda raced to my cage. While Miranda looked on the outside of the cage, Sayeh opened the door and reached inside.

'Humphrey, do you mind if I look in your cage?' she asked.

'Help yourself,' I said.

She gently poked around in the bedding.

'I found the treasure!' she said as she held up the chocolate coin.

Garth rushed to her side. He was looking VERY-VERY-VERY confused.

'That's not the treasure!' he said.

Garth reached into my cage and poked around some more. Then he turned to face

his friends.

'The real treasure is missing,' he said. 'This
is fake treasure.'

Sayeh looked unsqueakably confused.

Garth looked unsqueakably upset.

I was unsqueakably sorry that everybody
was so disappointed.

Mystery Solved

'What did you do with it, Humphrey?'
Garth asked me. 'Where did you hide it?'

'I didn't!' I squeaked. 'The thief took it.'

'Humphrey's just a hamster,' Garth's dad said. 'What could he do?'

'You don't know Humphrey,' Garth said.

Some of my friends laughed. They knew I'd had a lot of amazing adventures.

'Humphrey wouldn't do anything bad,' Miranda said.

'BOING!' Og added.

My other friends all agreed.

Garth shook his head. 'But how could the real treasure disappear like that? And how did the chocolate coin get into Humphrey's cage?'

'I'm happy with the treasure I found,' Sayeh said. 'Don't worry, Garth.'

But Garth was still upset. 'I don't know how that coin got in there. It was on my desk.'

'Do you think a thief came in and stole

your treasure?' Garth's mum smiled. 'And then replaced it? That's silly.'

'No, it's not!' I squeaked.

'Somebody could have taken it while we were searching,' Garth said. 'We weren't looking at Humphrey's cage the whole time.'

'True,' Garth's dad said.

'False!' I said. 'You're WRONG-WRONG-WRONG!'

Everybody laughed at my squeaking. I wish they'd at least try to understand me.

'Only Humphrey really knows what happened,' Miranda said.

She was almost right. Og and I were the only ones who knew that the thief had stolen the treasure the night before.

She didn't know that we had no idea who the thief was.

I thought about who it could have been.

The only humans who were in the house were Garth, his mum, his dad, Andy and A.J.

Garth wouldn't have taken his own treasure. If he had, wouldn't he have told me?

Garth's mum and dad were too nice to steal anything.

A.J. wasn't a thief. But had he been playing a joke on Garth?

And Andy had been asleep in bed when the treasure was stolen.

I looked at Garth's little brother.

He didn't look like a thief.

But he did look funny with chocolate smeared all over his face.

'Andy! I told you, no chocolate cake until

later!' Garth's mum said when she saw him.

'You sneaked some chocolate last night, too.'

'Yum, chocolate,' Andy said. 'YUM!'

Garth said, 'Sssh!'

Andy said, 'Sssh!' right back.

The thief had smelled like chocolate. Andy loved chocolate. And he'd been eating it last night.

The thief had said 'Sssh!' Garth and A.J. said 'Sssh!' But Andy liked to say 'Sssh!' a *lot*.

Andy had been in the house last night. But now I knew he hadn't been in bed.

I raced to the front of my cage.

'You did it, Andy! You're the thief,' I squeaked. 'Turn yourself in!'

All my friends giggled at my SQUEAK-SQUEAK-SQUEAKs. But I didn't giggle.

'Andy is the thief!' I said. 'He did it!'

'Humphrey seems mad at Andy,' Garth said.

'Yes, he does,' Garth's mum said.

She turned to Andy. 'Did you take the treasure out of Humphrey's cage?'

Andy looked down at the ground. 'Yes,' he said softly.

'Why?' Garth asked.

'I like treasure,' Andy said.

Garth had another question. 'And did you put the chocolate coin in the cage?'

'I like chocolate,' Andy said.

It wasn't a real answer, but Garth didn't notice.

'Go get the treasure,' Garth's dad said. '*Now!*'

Andy went into the house and soon came back carrying the little treasure chest.

'Give it to Sayeh,' Garth's mum told him. 'And tell her you're sorry.'

Andy handed Sayeh the chest.

'Sorry,' he said.

He looked REALLY-REALLY-REALLY
sorry, too.

Everyone gathered round while Sayeh
opened the tiny chest.

'Oh!' she said as she reached inside. 'It's a
gift card for Tilly's Toy Store!'

All my friends said, 'Oooh.'

Sayeh handed Andy the chocolate coin.
'This is for you, Andy. Because you told the
truth.'

Andy smiled happily, until his mum took the coin to save for later.

'Thanks for solving the mystery for us, Humphrey,' Garth's dad said. 'You're quite a treasure yourself.'

'BOING-BOING!' Og agreed.

'Og, you're a treasure, too,' Garth's dad laughed.

Garth's mum announced it was time for cake and ice cream so my friends ran off to the food table.

But Garth came straight back.

'Humphrey, I'm sorry I blamed you,' he said. 'I should have known that you'd never steal anything.'

He opened the door of my cage and put a small piece of carrot inside.

'Here's a treat for you,' he said.

Yum! That lovely orange carrot looked like sparkly golden treasure to me.

I hid it under the bedding in my cage for later on, when I'd have a treasure hunt all by myself.

'Thanks for making it a great party,' Garth said.

'You're welcome,' I replied. 'It was a GREAT-GREAT-GREAT party.'

And I REALLY-REALLY-REALLY meant it.

Humphrey and his friends have been hard at work making a brand new FUN-FUN-FUN website just for you!

Play Humphrey's exciting new game, share your pet pictures, find fun crafts and activities, read Humphrey's very own diary and discover all the latest news from your favourite furry friend at:

www.funwithhumphrey.com

A. A. MILNE

Tales from

Winnie-the-Pooh

WITH THE ORIGINAL LINE ILLUSTRATONS BY

E. H. SHEPARD

EGMONT

EGMONT

We bring stories to life

This edition first published in Great Britain in 2011
by Egmont UK Limited
239 Kensington High Street, London W8 6SA

Winnie-the-Pooh first published 1926 by Methuen & Co. Limited
Text by A. A. Milne copyright © Trustees of the Pooh Properties
Line illustrations copyright © E. H. Shepard

ISBN 978 0 9566276 3 6

1 3 5 7 9 10 8 6 4 2

Printed and bound in Great Britain by the CPI Group

DRAWN BY ME

TO NORTH POLE

BEE
TREE

BIG
STONES
AND
ROX

RABBITS
FRENDS AND
RALETIONS

MY
HOUSE

OWLS
HOUSE

100 AKER
WOOD

EEYORES
GLOOMY
PLACE

RATHER BOGGY
AND SAD

AND MR SHEPARD HELPD

CHAPTER ONE

In which Pooh and Piglet go hunting and nearly catch a Woozle

The Piglet lived in a very grand house in the middle of a beech-tree, and the beech-tree was in the middle of the Forest, and the Piglet lived in the middle of the house. Next to his house was a piece of broken board which had: "TRESPASSERS W" on it. When Christopher Robin asked the Piglet what it meant, he said it was his grandfather's name, and had been in the

family for a long time. Christopher Robin said you *couldn't* be called Trespassers W, and Piglet said yes, you could, because his grandfather was, and it was short for

Trespassers Will, which was short for Trespassers William. And his grandfather had had two names in case he lost one – Trespassers after an uncle, and William after Trespassers.

"I've got two names," said Christopher Robin carelessly.

"Well, there you are, that proves it," said Piglet.

One fine winter's day when Piglet was brushing away the snow in front of his house, he happened to look up, and there was Winnie-the-Pooh. Pooh was walking round and round in a circle, thinking of something else, and when Piglet called to him, he just went on walking.

"Hallo!" said Piglet, "what are *you* doing?"

"Hunting," said Pooh.

"Hunting what?"

"Tracking something," said Winnie-the-Pooh very mysteriously.

"Tracking what?" said Piglet, coming closer.

"That's just what I ask myself. I ask myself, What?"

"What do you think you'll answer?"

"I shall have to wait until I catch up with it," said Winnie-the-Pooh. "Now, look there." He pointed to the ground in front of him. "What do you see there?"

"Tracks," said Piglet, "Paw-marks." He gave a little squeak of excitement. "Oh, Pooh! Do you think it's a – a – a Woozle?"

"It may be," said Pooh. "Sometimes it is, and sometimes it isn't. You never can tell with paw-marks."

With these few words he went on

tracking, and Piglet, after watching him for a minute or two, ran after him. Winnie-the-Pooh had come to a sudden stop, and was bending over the tracks in a puzzled sort of way.

"What's the matter?" asked Piglet.

"It's a very funny thing," said Bear, "but there seem to be *two* animals now. This – whatever-it-was – has been joined by another – whatever-it-is – and the two

of them are now proceeding in company. Would you mind coming with me, Piglet, in case they turn out to be Hostile Animals?"

Piglet scratched his ear in a nice sort of way, and said that he had nothing to do until Friday, and would be delighted to come, in case it really *was* a Woozle.

"You mean, in case it really is two Woozles," said Winnie-the-Pooh, and Piglet said that anyhow he had nothing to do until Friday. So off they went together.

There was a small spinney of larch-trees just here, and it seemed as if the two Woozles, if that is what they were, had been going round this spinney; so round this spinney went Pooh and Piglet after them; Piglet passing the time by telling Pooh what his Grandfather Trespassers W had done to Remove Stiffness after Tracking, and how

12

his Grandfather Trespassers W had suffered in his later years from Shortness of Breath, and other matters of interest, and Pooh wondering what a Grandfather was like, and if perhaps this was Two Grandfathers they were after now, and, if so, whether he would be allowed to take one home and keep it, and what Christopher Robin would say. And still the tracks went on in front of them . . .

Suddenly Winnie-the-Pooh stopped, and pointed excitedly in front of him. "*Look!*"

"*What?*" said Piglet, with a jump. And then, to show that he hadn't been frightened, he jumped up and down once or twice more in an exercising sort of way.

"The tracks!" said Pooh. "*A third animal has joined the other two!*"

"Pooh!" cried Piglet. "Do you think it is

another Woozle?"

"No," said Pooh, "because it makes different marks. It is either Two Woozles and one, as it might be Wizzle, or Two, as it might be, Wizzles and one, if so it is, Woozle. Let us continue to follow them."

So they went on, feeling just a little anxious now, in case the three animals in front of them were of Hostile Intent.

And Piglet wished very much that his Grandfather T. W. were there, instead of elsewhere, and Pooh thought how nice it would be if they met Christopher Robin suddenly but quite accidentally, and only because he liked Christopher Robin so much. And then, all of a sudden, Winnie-the-Pooh stopped again, and licked the tip of his nose in a cooling manner, for he was feeling more hot and anxious than ever in his life before. *There were four animals in front of them!*

"Do you see, Piglet? Look at their tracks! Three, as it were, Woozles, and one, as it was, Wizzle. *Another Woozle has joined them!*"

And so it seemed to be. There were the tracks; crossing over each other here, getting muddled up with each other there;

but, quite plainly every now and then, the tracks of four sets of paws.

"I *think*," said Piglet, when he had licked the tip of his nose too, and found that it brought very little comfort, "I *think* that I have just remembered something. I have just remembered something that I forgot to do yesterday and shan't be able to do to-morrow. So I suppose I really ought to go back and do it now."

"We'll do it this afternoon, and I'll come

with you," said Pooh.

"It isn't the sort of thing you can do in the afternoon," said Piglet quickly. "It's a very particular morning thing, that has to be done in the morning, and, if possible, between the hours of – What would you say the time was?"

"About twelve," said Winnie-the-Pooh, looking at the sun.

"Between, as I was saying, the hours of twelve and twelve five. So, really, dear old Pooh, if you'll excuse me – *What's that?*"

Pooh looked up at the sky, and then, as he heard the whistle again, he looked up into the branches of a big oak-tree, and then he saw a friend of his.

"It's Christopher Robin," he said. "Ah, then you'll be all right," said Piglet. "You'll be quite safe with *him*. Good-bye,"

and he trotted off home as quickly as he could, very glad to be Out of All Danger again.

Christopher Robin came slowly down his tree.

"Silly old Bear," he said, "what *were* you doing? First you went round the spinney twice by yourself, and then Piglet ran after you and you went round again together, and then you were just going round a fourth time —"

"Wait a moment," said Winnie-the-Pooh, holding up his paw.

He sat down and thought, in the most thoughtful way he could think. Then he fitted his paw into one of the Tracks . . . and then he scratched his nose twice, and stood up.

"Yes," said Winnie-the-Pooh.

"I see now," said Winnie-the-Pooh.

"I have been Foolish and Deluded," said he, "and I am a Bear of No Brain at All."

"You're the Best Bear in All the World," said Christopher Robin soothingly.

"Am I?" said Pooh hopefully. And then he brightened up suddenly.

"Anyhow," he said, "it is nearly Luncheon Time."

So he went home for it.

CHAPTER TWO

In which Eeyore has a birthday and gets two presents

Eeyore, the old grey Donkey, stood by the side of the stream, and looked at himself in the water.

"Pathetic," he said. "That's what it is. Pathetic."

He turned and walked slowly down the stream for twenty yards, splashed across it, and walked slowly back on the other side. Then he looked at himself in the water again.

"As I thought," he said. "No better from *this* side. But nobody minds. Nobody cares. Pathetic, that's what it is."

There was a crackling noise in the bracken behind him, and out came Pooh.

"Good morning, Eeyore," said Pooh.

"Good morning, Pooh Bear," said Eeyore gloomily. "If it *is* a good morning," he said. "Which I doubt," said he.

"Why, what's the matter?"

"Nothing, Pooh Bear, nothing. We can't all, and some of us don't. That's all there is to it."

"Can't all *what*?" said Pooh, rubbing his nose.

"Gaiety. Song-and-dance. Here we go round the mulberry bush."

"Oh!" said Pooh. He thought for a long time, and then asked, "What mulberry bush

25

is that?"

"Bon-hommy," went on Eeyore gloomily.
"French word meaning bonhommy," he
explained. "I'm not complaining, but There
It Is."

Pooh sat down on a large stone, and tried
to think this out. It sounded to him like
a riddle, and he was never much good at
riddles, being a Bear of Very Little Brain.
So he sang *Cottleston Pie* instead:

Cottleston, Cottleston, Cottleston Pie,
A fly can't bird, but a bird can fly.
Ask me a riddle and I reply:
"Cottleston, Cottleston, Cottleston Pie."

That was the first verse. When he had finished it, Eeyore didn't actually say that he didn't like it, so Pooh very kindly sang the second verse to him:

Cottleston, Cottleston, Cottleston Pie,
A fish can't whistle and neither can I.
Ask me a riddle and I reply:
"Cottleston, Cottleston, Cottleston Pie."

Eeyore still said nothing at all, so Pooh hummed the third verse quietly to himself:

Cottleston, Cottleston, Cottleston Pie,
Why does a chicken, I don't know why.
Ask me a riddle and I reply:
"Cottleston, Cottleston, Cottleston Pie."

"That's right," said Eeyore. "Sing. Umty-tiddly, umpty-too. Here we go gathering Nuts and May. Enjoy yourself."

"I am," said Pooh.

"Some can," said Eeyore.

"Why, what's the matter?"

"*Is* anything the matter?"

"You seem so sad, Eeyore."

"Sad? Why should I be sad? It's my birthday. The happiest day of the year."

"Your birthday?" said Pooh in great surprise.

"Of course it is. Can't you see? Look at all the presents I have had." He waved a foot from side to side.

"Look at the birthday cake. Candles and pink sugar."

Pooh looked – first to the right and then to the left.

"Presents?" said Pooh. "Birthday cake?" said Pooh. *Where?*

"Can't you see them?"

"No," said Pooh.

"Neither can I," said Eeyore. "Joke," he explained. "Ha ha!"

Pooh scratched his head, being a little

puzzled by all this.

"But is it really your birthday?" he asked.

"It is."

"Oh! Well, many happy returns of the day, Eeyore."

"And many happy returns to you, Pooh Bear."

"But it isn't *my* birthday."

"No, it's mine."

"But you said 'Many happy returns' —"

"Well, why not? You don't always want to be miserable on my birthday, do you?"

"Oh I see," said Pooh.

"It's bad enough," said Eeyore, almost breaking down, "being miserable myself, what with no presents and no cake and no candles, and no proper notice taken of me at all, but if everybody else is going to be miserable too —"

This was too much for Pooh. "Stay there!" he called to Eeyore, as he turned and hurried back home as quick as he could; for he felt that he must get poor Eeyore a present of *some* sort at once, and he could always think of a proper one afterwards.

Outside his house he found Piglet, jumping up and down trying to reach the knocker.

"Hallo, Piglet," he said.

"Hallo, Pooh," said Piglet.

"What are *you* trying to do?"

"I was trying to reach the knocker," said Piglet. "I just came round –"

"Let me do it for you," said Pooh kindly. So he reached up and knocked at the door. "I have just seen Eeyore," he began, "and poor Eeyore is in a Very Sad Condition, because it's his birthday, and nobody has taken any notice of it, and he's very Gloomy – you know what Eeyore is – and there he was, and – What a long time whoever lives here is answering this door."

And he knocked again.

"But Pooh," said Piglet, "it's your own house!"

"Oh!" said Pooh. "So it is," he said. "Well, let's go in."

So in they went. The first thing Pooh did was to go to the cupboard to see if he had quite a small jar of honey left; and he had, so he took it down.

"I'm giving this to Eeyore," he explained, "as a present. What are *you* going to give?"

"Couldn't I give it too?" said Piglet. "From both of us?"

"No," said Pooh. "That would *not* be a good plan."

"All right, then, I'll give him a balloon. I've got one left from my party. I'll go and

get it now, shall I?"

"That, Piglet, is a *very* good idea. It is just what Eeyore wants to cheer him up. Nobody can be uncheered with a balloon."

So off Piglet trotted; and in the other direction went Pooh, with his jar of honey.

It was a warm day, and he had a long way to go. He hadn't gone more than half-way when a sort of funny feeling began to creep all over him. It began at the tip of his nose and trickled all through him and out at the soles of his feet. It was just as if somebody inside him were saying, "Now then, Pooh, time for a little something."

"Dear, dear," said Pooh, "I didn't know it was as late as that." So he sat down and took the top off his jar of honey. "Lucky I

brought this with me," he thought. "Many a bear going out on a warm day like this would never have thought of bringing a little something with him." And he began to eat.

"Now let me see," he thought, as he took

his last lick of the inside of the jar, "where was I going? Ah, yes, Eeyore." He got up slowly.

And then, suddenly, he remembered. He had eaten Eeyore's birthday present!

"*Bother!*" said Pooh. "What *shall* I do? I *must* give him *something*."

For a little while he couldn't think of anything. Then he thought: "Well, it's a very nice pot, even if there's no honey in it, and if I washed it clean, and got somebody to write '*A Happy Birthday*' on it, Eeyore could keep things in it, which might be Useful." So, as he was just passing the Hundred Acre Wood, he went inside to call on Owl, who lived there.

"Good morning, Owl," he said.

"Good morning, Pooh," said Owl.

"Many happy returns of Eeyore's

birthday," said Pooh.

"Oh, is that what it is?"

"What are you giving him, Owl?"

"What are *you* giving him, Pooh?"

"I'm giving him a Useful Pot to Keep Things In, and I wanted to ask you –"

"Is this it?" said Owl, taking it out of Pooh's paw.

"Yes, and I wanted to ask you –"

"Somebody has been keeping honey in it," said Owl.

"You can keep *anything* in it," said Pooh earnestly. "It's Very Useful like that. And I wanted to ask you –"

"You ought to write *'A Happy Birthday'* on it."

"*That* was what I wanted to ask you," said Pooh. "Because my spelling is Wobbly. It's good spelling but it Wobbles, and the

letters get in the wrong places. Would *you* write 'A Happy Birthday' on it for me?"

"It's a nice pot," said Owl, looking at it all round. "Couldn't I give it too? From both of us?"

"No," said Pooh. "That would *not* be a good plan. Now I'll just wash it first, and then you can write on it."

Well, he washed the pot out, and dried it, while Owl licked the end of his pencil, and wondered how to spell 'birthday'.

"Can you read, Pooh?" he asked a little anxiously. "There's a notice about knocking and ringing outside my door, which Christopher Robin wrote. Could you read it?"

"Christopher Robin told me what it said, and *then* I could."

"Well, I'll tell you what *this* says, and then you"ll be able to."

So Owl wrote . . . and this is what he wrote:

HIPY PAPY BTHUTHDTH
THUTHDA
BTHUTHDY.

Pooh looked on admiringly.

"I'm just saying 'A Happy Birthday'," said Owl carelessly.

"It's a nice long one," said Pooh, very much impressed by it.

"Well, *actually*, of course, I'm saying 'A very Happy Birthday with love from Pooh.' Naturally it takes a good deal of pencil to say a long thing like that."

"Oh, I see," said Pooh.

While all this was happening, Piglet had gone back to his own house to get Eeyore's balloon. He held it very tightly against himself, so that it shouldn't blow away, and he ran as fast as he could so as to get to Eeyore before Pooh did; for he thought that he would like to be the first one to give a present, just as if he had thought of it without being told by anybody.

And running along,

40

and thinking how pleased Eeyore would be, he didn't look where he was going . . . and suddenly he put his foot in a rabbit hole, and fell down flat on his face.

BANG!!!???***!!!

Piglet lay there, wondering what had happened. At first he thought that the whole world had blown up; and then he thought that perhaps only the Forest part of it had; and then he thought that perhaps only *he* had, and he was now alone in the moon or somewhere, and would never see Christopher Robin or Pooh or Eeyore again. And then he thought, "Well, even if I'm in the moon, I needn't be face downwards all the time," so he got cautiously up and

looked about him.

He was still in the Forest!

"Well, that's funny," he thought. "I wonder what that bang was. I couldn't have made such a noise just falling down. And where's my balloon? And what's that small piece of damp rag doing?"

It was the balloon!

"Oh, dear!" said Piglet. "Oh, dear, oh, dearie, dearie, dear! Well, it's too late now. I can't go back, and I haven't another balloon, and perhaps Eeyore doesn't *like* balloons so *very* much."

So he trotted on, rather sadly now, and down he came to the side of the stream where Eeyore was, and called out to him.

"Good morning, Eeyore," shouted Piglet.

"Good morning, Little Piglet," said Eeyore. "If it *is* a good morning," he said.

"Which I doubt," said he. "Not that it matters," he said.

"Many happy returns of the day," said Piglet, having now got closer.

Eeyore stopped looking at himself in the stream, and turned to stare at Piglet.

"Just say that again," he said.

"Many hap –"

"Wait a moment."

Balancing on three legs, he began to bring his fourth leg very cautiously up to his ear. "I did this yesterday," he explained, as he fell down for the third time. "It's quite easy. It's so as I can hear better . . . There, that's

done it! Now then, what were you saying?"
He pushed his ear forward with his hoof.

"Many happy returns of the day," said
Piglet again.

"Meaning me?"

"Of course, Eeyore."

"My birthday?"

"Yes."

"Me having a real birthday?"

"Yes, Eeyore, and I've brought you a
present."

Eeyore took down his right hoof from
his right ear, turned round, and with great
difficulty put up his left hoof.

"I must have that in the other ear," he
said. "Now then."

"A present," said Piglet very loudly.

"Meaning me again?"

"Yes."

"My birthday still?"

"Of course, Eeyore."

"Me going on having a real birthday?"

"Yes, Eeyore, and I brought you a balloon."

"*Balloon?*" said Eeyore. "You did say balloon? One of those big coloured things you blow up? Gaiety, song-and-dance, here we are and there we are?"

"Yes, but I'm afraid – I'm very sorry, Eeyore – but when I was running along to bring it you, I fell down."

"Dear, dear, how unlucky! You ran too fast, I expect. You didn't hurt yourself, Little Piglet?"

"No, but I – I – oh, Eeyore, I burst the balloon!"

There was a very long silence.

"My balloon?" said Eeyore at last.

Piglet nodded.

"My birthday balloon?"

"Yes, Eeyore," said Piglet, sniffing a little. "Here it is. With – with many happy returns of the day." And he gave Eeyore the small piece of damp rag.

"Is this it?" said Eeyore, a little surprised.

Piglet nodded.

"My present?"

Piglet nodded again.

"The balloon?"

"Yes."

"Thank you, Piglet," said Eeyore. "You

don't mind my asking," he went on, "but what colour was this balloon when it — when it *was* a balloon?"

"Red."

"I just wondered . . . Red," he murmured to himself. "My favourite colour . . . How big was it?"

"About as big as me."

"I just wondered . . . About as big as Piglet," he said to himself sadly. "My favourite size. Well, well."

Piglet felt very miserable, and didn't know what to say. He was still opening his mouth to begin something, and then deciding that it wasn't any good saying *that*, when he heard a shout from the other side of the river, and there was Pooh.

"Many happy returns of the day," called out Pooh, forgetting that he had said it

already.

"Thank you, Pooh, I'm having them," said Eeyore gloomily.

"I've brought you a little present," said Pooh excitedly.

"I've had it," said Eeyore.

Pooh had now splashed across the stream to Eeyore, and Piglet was sitting a little way off, his head in his paws, snuffling to himself.

"It's a Useful Pot," said Pooh. "Here it is. And it's got 'A Very Happy Birthday with love from Pooh' written on it. That's what all that writing is. And it's for putting things in. There!"

When Eeyore saw the pot, he became quite excited. "Why!" he said. "I believe my Balloon will just go into that Pot!"

"Oh, no, Eeyore," said Pooh. "Balloons

are much too big to go into Pots. What you do with a balloon is, you hold the balloon –"

"Not mine," said Eeyore proudly. "Look, Piglet!" And as Piglet looked sorrowfully round, Eeyore picked the balloon up with his teeth, and placed it carefully in the pot; picked it out and put it on the ground; and then picked it up again and put it carefully back.

"So it does!" said Pooh. "It goes in!"

"So it does!" said Piglet. "And it comes out!"

"Doesn't it?" said Eeyore. "It goes in and out like anything."

"I'm very glad," said Pooh happily, "that I thought of giving you a Useful Pot to put things in."

"I'm very glad," said Piglet happily, "that

I thought of giving you Something to put in a Useful Pot."

But Eeyore wasn't listening. He was taking the balloon out, and putting it back again, as happy as could be . . .

"And didn't *I* give him anything?" asked Christopher Robin sadly.

"Of course you did," I said. "You gave him – don't you remember – a little – a little –"

"I gave him a box of paints to paint things with."

"That was it."

"Why didn't I give it to him in the morning?"

"You were so busy getting his party ready for him. He had a cake with icing on the top, and three candles, and his name in pink sugar, and –"

"Yes, *I* remember," said Christopher Robin.

CHAPTER THREE

In which Piglet is entirely surrounded by water

It rained and it rained and it rained. Piglet told himself that never in all his life, and *he* was goodness knows *how* old – three, was it, or four? – never had he seen so much rain. Days and days and days.

"If only," he thought, as he looked out of the window, "I had been in Pooh's house, or Christopher Robin's house, or Rabbit's house when it began to rain, then I should have had Company all this time, instead

of being here all alone, with nothing to do except wonder when it will stop." And he imagined himself with Pooh, saying, "Did you ever see such rain, Pooh?" and Pooh saying, "Isn't it *awful*, Piglet?" and Piglet saying, "I wonder how it is over Christopher Robin's way," and Pooh saying, "I should think poor old Rabbit is about flooded out by this time." It would have been jolly to talk like this, and really, it wasn't much good having anything exciting like floods, if you couldn't share them with somebody.

For it was rather exciting. The little dry ditches in which Piglet had nosed about so often had become streams, the little streams across which he had splashed were rivers, and the river, between whose steep banks they had played so happily, had sprawled out of its own bed and was taking up so

much room everywhere, that Piglet was beginning to wonder whether it would be coming into *his* bed soon.

"It's a little Anxious," he said to himself, "to be a Very Small Animal Entirely Surrounded by Water. Christopher Robin and Pooh could escape by Climbing Trees, and Kanga could escape by Jumping, and Rabbit could escape by Burrowing, and Owl could escape by Flying, and Eeyore could escape by – by Making a Loud Noise Until Rescued, and here am I, surrounded by water and I can't do *anything*."

It went on raining, and every day the water got a little higher, until now it was nearly up to Piglet's window . . . and still he hadn't done anything.

"There's Pooh," he thought to himself. "Pooh hasn't much Brain, but he never

comes to any harm. He does silly things and they turn out right. There's Owl. Owl hasn't exactly got Brain, but he Knows Things. He would know the Right Thing to Do when Surrounded by Water. There's Rabbit. He hasn't Learnt in Books, but he can always Think of a Clever Plan. There's Kanga. She isn't Clever, Kanga isn't, but she would be so anxious about Roo that she would do a Good Thing to Do without thinking about it. And then there's Eeyore. And Eeyore is so miserable anyhow that he wouldn't mind about this. But I wonder what Christopher Robin would do?"

Then suddenly he remembered a story which Christopher Robin had told him about a man on a desert island who had written something in a bottle and thrown it into the sea; and Piglet thought that if he

wrote something in a bottle and threw it in the water, perhaps somebody would come and rescue *him*!

He left the window and began to search his house, all of it that wasn't under water, and at last he found a pencil and a small piece of dry paper, and a bottle with a cork to it. And he wrote on one side of the paper:

HELP!
PIGLIT (ME)

and on the other side:

IT'S ME PIGLIT, HELP HELP!

Then he put the paper in the bottle, and he corked the bottle up as tightly as he could, and he leant out of his window as far as he

could lean without falling in, and he threw
the bottle as far as he could throw – *splash!*
– and in a little while it bobbed up again on
the water; and he watched it floating slowly
away in the distance, until his eyes ached
with looking, and sometimes he thought it
was the bottle, and sometimes he thought it
was just a ripple on the water which he was
following, and then suddenly he knew that
he would never see it again and that he had
done all that he could do to save himself.

"So now," he thought, "somebody else

will have to do something, and I hope they will do it soon, because if they don't I shall have to swim, which I can't, so I hope they do it soon." And then he gave a very long sigh and said, "I wish Pooh were here. It's so much more friendly with two."

When the rain began Pooh was asleep. It rained, and it rained, and it rained, and he slept and he slept and he slept. He had had a tiring day. You remember how he discovered the North Pole; well, he was so proud of this that he asked Christopher Robin if there were any other Poles such as a Bear of Little Brain might discover.

"There's a South Pole," said Christopher Robin, "and I expect there's an East Pole and a West Pole, though people don't like talking about them."

Pooh was very excited when he heard this, and suggested that they should have an Expotition to discover the East Pole, but Christopher Robin had thought of something else to do with Kanga; so Pooh went out to discover the East Pole by himself. Whether he discovered it or not, I forget; but he was so tired when he got home that, in the very middle of his supper, after he had been eating for little more than half-an-hour, he fell fast asleep in his chair, and slept and slept and slept.

Then suddenly he was dreaming. He was at the East Pole, and it was a very cold pole with the coldest sort of snow and ice all over it. He had found a beehive to sleep in, but there wasn't room for his legs, so he had left them outside. And Wild Woozles, such as inhabit the East Pole, came and nibbled all

the fur off his legs to make Nests for their Young. And the more they nibbled, the colder his legs got, until suddenly he woke up with an *Ow!* – and there he was, sitting in his chair with his feet in the water, and water all round him!

He splashed to his door and looked out . . .

"This is Serious," said Pooh. "I must have an Escape."

So he took his largest pot of honey and escaped with it to a broad branch of his tree, well above the water, and then he climbed down again and escaped with another pot . . . and when the whole Escape was finished, there was Pooh sitting on his branch, dangling his legs, and there, beside him, were ten pots of honey . . .

Two days later, there was Pooh, sitting

on his branch, dangling his legs, and there beside him, were four pots of honey.

Three days later, there was Pooh, sitting on his branch, dangling his legs, and there beside him, was one pot of honey . . .

Four days later, there was Pooh . . .

And it was on the morning of the fourth day that Piglet's bottle came floating past him, and with one loud cry of "Honey!"

Pooh plunged into the water, seized the bottle, and struggled back to his tree again.

"Bother!" said Pooh, as he opened it. "All that wet for nothing. What's that bit of paper doing?"

He took it out and looked.

"It's a Missage," he said to himself, "that's what it is. And that letter is a 'P', and so is that, and so is that, and 'P' means 'Pooh', so it's a very important Missage to me, and I can't read it. I must find Christopher Robin or Owl or Piglet, one of those Clever Readers who can read things, and they will tell me what this missage means. Only I can't swim. Bother!"

Then he had an idea, and I think that for a Bear of Very Little Brain, it was a good idea. He said to himself:

"If a bottle can float, then a jar can float,

and if a jar floats, I can sit on the top of it, if it's a very big jar."

So he took his biggest jar, and corked it up.

"All boats have to have a name," he said, "so I shall call mine *The Floating Bear*." And with these words he dropped his boat into the water and jumped in after it.

For a little while Pooh and *The Floating Bear* were uncertain as to which of them was meant to be on the top, but after trying

one or two different positions, they settled
down with *The Floating Bear* underneath

and Pooh triumphantly astride it, paddling
vigorously with his feet.

Christopher Robin lived at the very top of the Forest. It rained, and it rained, and it rained, but the water couldn't come up to *his* house. It was rather jolly to look down into the valleys and see the water all round him, but it rained so hard that he stayed indoors most of the time, and thought about things. Every morning he went out with his umbrella and put a stick in the place where the water came up to, and every next morning he went out and couldn't see his

stick any more, so he put another stick in the place where the water came up to, and then he walked home again, and each morning he had a shorter way to walk than he had had the morning before. On the morning of the fifth day he saw the water all round him, and knew that for the first time in his life he was on a real island. Which was very exciting.

It was on this morning that Owl came flying over the water to say "How do you do?" to his friend Christopher Robin.

"I say, Owl," said Christopher Robin, "isn't this fun? I'm on an island!"

"The atmospheric conditions have been very unfavourable lately," said Owl.

"The what?"

"It has been raining," explained Owl.

"Yes," said Christopher Robin. "It has."

"The flood-level has reached an unprecedented height."

"The who?"

"There's a lot of water about," explained Owl.

"Yes," said Christopher Robin, "there is."

"However, the prospects are rapidly becoming more favourable. At any moment –"

"Have you seen Pooh?"

"No. At any moment –"

"I hope he's all right," said Christopher Robin. "I've been wondering about him. I expect Piglet's with him. Do you think they're all right, Owl?"

"I expect so. You see, at any moment –"

"Do go and see, Owl. Because Pooh hasn't got very much brain, and he might do something silly, and I do love him so,

Owl. Do you see, Owl?"

"That's all right," said Owl. "I'll go. Back directly." And he flew off.

In a little while he was back again.

"Pooh isn't there," he said.

"Not there?"

"He's *been* there. He's been sitting on a branch of his tree outside his house with nine pots of honey. But he isn't there now."

"Oh, Pooh!" cried Christopher Robin. "Where *are* you?"

"Here I am," said a growly voice behind him.

"Pooh!"

They rushed into each other's arms.

"How did you get here, Pooh?" asked Christopher Robin, when he was ready to talk again.

"On my boat," said Pooh proudly.

"I had a Very Important Missage sent me in a bottle, and owing to having got some water in my eyes, I couldn't read it, so I brought it to you. On my boat."

With these proud words he gave Christopher Robin the missage.

"But it's from Piglet!" cried Christopher Robin when he had read it.

"Isn't there anything about Pooh in it?" asked Bear, looking over his shoulder.

Christopher Robin read the message aloud.

"Oh, are those 'P's' piglets? I thought they were Poohs."

"We must rescue him at once! I thought he was with *you*, Pooh. Owl, could you rescue him on your back?"

"I don't think so," said Owl, after grave thought. "It is doubtful if the necessary dorsal muscles —"

71

"Then would you fly to him at *once* and say that Rescue is Coming? And Pooh and I will think of a Rescue and come as quick as ever we can. Oh, don't *talk*, Owl, go on quick!" And, still thinking of something to say, Owl flew off.

"Now then, Pooh," said Christopher Robin, "where's your boat?"

"I ought to say," explained Pooh as they walked down to the shore of the island, "that it isn't just an ordinary sort of boat. Sometimes it's a Boat, and sometimes it's more of an Accident. It all depends."

"Depends on what?"

"On whether I'm on the top of it or underneath it."

"Oh! Well, where is it?"

"There!" said Pooh, pointing proudly to *The Floating Bear*.

It wasn't what Christopher Robin
expected, and the more he looked at it, the
more he thought what a Brave and Clever
Bear Pooh was, and the more Christopher
Robin thought this, the more Pooh looked
modestly down his nose and tried to pretend
he wasn't.

"But it's too small for two of us," said
Christopher Robin sadly.

"Three of us with Piglet."

"That makes it smaller still. Oh, Pooh
Bear, what shall we do?"

And then this Bear, Pooh Bear, Winnie-
the-Pooh, F.O.P. (Friend of Piglet's),
R.C. (Rabbit's Companion), P.D. (Pole
Discoverer), E.C. and T.F. (Eeyore's
Comforter and Tail-finder) – in fact,
Pooh himself – said something so clever
that Christopher Robin could only look

at him with mouth open and eyes staring, wondering if this was really the Bear of Very Little Brain whom he had known and loved so long.

"We might go in your umbrella," said Pooh.

"?"

"We might go in your umbrella," said Pooh.

"??"

"We might go in your umbrella," said Pooh.

"!!!!!!"

For suddenly Christopher Robin saw that they might. He opened his umbrella and put it point downwards in the water. It floated but wobbled. Pooh got in. He was just beginning to say that it was all right now, when he found that it wasn't, so after

a short drink, which he didn't really want, he waded back to Christopher Robin. Then they both got in together, and it wobbled no longer.

"I shall call this boat *The Brain of Pooh*," said Christopher Robin, and *The Brain of Pooh* set sail forthwith in a south-westerly direction, revolving gracefully.

You can imagine Piglet's joy when at last the ship came in sight of him. In after-years he liked to think that he had been in Very Great Danger during the Terrible Flood,

but the only danger he had really been in was the last half-hour of his imprisonment, when Owl, who had just flown up, sat on a branch of his tree to comfort him, and told him a very long story about an aunt who had once laid a seagull's egg by mistake, and the story went on and on, rather like this sentence, until Piglet who was listening out of his window without much hope, went to sleep quietly and naturally, slipping slowly

out of the window towards the water until
he was only hanging on by his toes, at which
moment, luckily, a sudden loud squawk
from Owl, which was really part of the story,
being what his aunt said, woke the Piglet up
and just gave him time to jerk himself back

into safety and say, "How interesting, and
did she?" when — well you can imagine his
joy when at last he saw the good ship, *Brain
of Pooh* (*Captain*, C. Robin; *1st Mate*, P. Bear)
coming over the sea to rescue him . . .

And as that is really the end of the story, and I am very tired after that last sentence, I think I shall stop there.